75 Fun Stories fo

3 to 8 Year Olds

What Will You Find Here?

Do you love reading Fun stories? Well, this eBook has lots of interesting stories for you. You can find stories on action, adventure, importance of good habits, friendship, pets, and having fun with family. You can also read this eBook with your friends and have fun. Let's get started and see what all do we have here.

Contents

Peter Goes to the Dentist

It was a bright Saturday afternoon. The day for little Peter's dentist appointment had finally arrived. He was watching TV when his mom told him it was time to go. He quickly got dressed and was ready for his first appointment with the dentist.

Little Peter sat in the back seat of the car with his little sister Jenny as mom drove them to the doctor's clinic. Little Peter was very excited as it was a new experience from him. He strolled inside and took a seat outside the doctor's office eagerly waiting his turn. Finally, the bell rang and Peter was next in line, his mother accompanied him inside along with the baby.

Upon entering the room, Peter's eyes lit up as he saw the dentist who greeted him politely and asked him to sit on the chair. At first, Peter was a bit scared after seeing all the equipment in the room but Doctor Mike reassured him and eased his fears.

After a short while the checkup was complete and Peter returned home with his family. That day he had learned a valuable lesson about dental care and why it is important to keep his teeth clean.

Tom's First Day at School

Tom was a very patient young boy. He was very helpful to others and was a hardworking student. When Tom's family moved houses he had to leave his old school and move to a new one. Tom's family arrived in the new town and soon Tom was enrolled into the local elementary school.

Tom was a little scared going to the new school as he did not know anyone there. However, his mom assured him that it would be fun and he would make a lot of friends. Soon it was time to go to school and as dad drove Tom to school he looked on with hope in his eyes. Soon they reached the campus and went inside. Tom was taken to the classroom by his dad where he would meet his class teacher.

Tom and dad waited for the teacher's arrival while Tom admired the beautiful drawings on the soft boards. Miss Martha entered the room and looked upon Tom with love. She met dad and talked with him for a while. Miss Martha's friendly attitude had already won Tom over. He happily attended the classes that day and made a few friends as well.

The Camping Trip

Spring was finally here and John was ready for his big camping trip with Uncle Ben. John was dressed in his favorite bright yellow shirt and grey shorts. Soon the bell rang and John ran towards the door in anticipation, he was glad to see his Uncle who greeted him warmly.

After completing the preparations, Uncle Ben and John were ready to go. As they sat in the car, John's mother shouted "Have you taken the umbrella?" She yelled. John replied "yes mother!" He was in such a hurry that he didn't bother checking.

It was almost night time when they reached the campsite. So Uncle Ben quickly set up the camp and started the fire as they prepared for the night ahead. The weather was very cloudy at night and soon it started raining cats and dogs. Uncle Ben asked John for the umbrella but he had forgotten it at home.

Soaked with water, they rushed back home in the car as the rain began to pour down. Eventually they made it back safely. John then realized that he had made a mistake that day which could have been easily avoided had he listened to his mother. John vowed that from that day on he would always listen to advice from his elders.

The Prince in Disguise

Prince Edward was a charming young man. He always helped the poor and needy in his kingdom. His father, King George, was exactly the opposite. He was a harsh man who was very unforgiving. One day the prince grew frustrated with his father's attitude and planned to live as a commoner.

Prince Edward escaped the castle at night and disguised himself in common clothes. The very next morning the king and queen were told of his escape by the guards. They instantly sent their men to search for him but even after days they couldn't find him. The queen was worried for her son and offered a reward of 100 gold coins to anyone who would bring him back.

Prince Edward had heard the news and he saw this as an opportunity to help the poor. Soon the prince rushed back to the kingdom and took off his disguise. Both the king and queen were delighted to see him and were ready to accept his demands.

The prince asked his father to distribute the gold among the poor and also provide them with food. The King had realized his mistake and apologized to the people of the land. He thanked the prince for showing him the light and they lived happily ever after.

Joe the Money Collector

Joe was a very clever boy. He was very mischievous and would always trouble his teachers at school. One day he came up with a plan to earn some money by fooling others. Together with his elder cousin Mike he planned to sell fake cola to the other children at school.

Mike and Joe tricked the kids by claiming that it was a special cola and charged twice the money. They had made the drink themselves by just mixing lemonade, ice and orange juice. It looked so good that everyone was easily deceived. The children rushed to the stall and instantly bought the drinks.

The taste was sour and the children were not happy at all. They wanted their money back, but by that time both Joe and Mike had escaped with their money. However, their trickery wouldn't last for long as the school principal soon took action. He called the parents of both the children for a meeting and informed them of their children's acts.

Joe's parents were ashamed. They couldn't believe that Joe could do such a thing. They immediately asked him to return the money and apologize. Joe had learned a life lesson that day that you must never trick others. Joe vowed to never do such a thing ever again.

The Monkey Brothers

One day Paul the monkey and his 5 other brothers were very hungry. They had not eaten since morning and mama monkey was out for work. The brothers decided to find food themselves. They searched and searched but couldn't find anything to eat.

Then all of a sudden Paul the monkey spotted a big tree full of fresh bananas. He quickly went to his brothers and told them. They all rushed to the tree in sheer excitement. They were overjoyed by the sight of bananas. However, soon their joy was cut short as Jimmy, the eldest monkey, realized that the tree was too hard to climb. But soon the monkey brothers found a friend who helped them. Minnie the bird told them that they could climb the tree if they all climbed on top of one another.

Even after failing at the first few attempts, the monkey brothers did not give up. They worked together as a team and eventually reached the banana branch. Jimmy pulled down the bananas for his brothers and then they ate peacefully. The brothers thanked Minnie for her help and danced in celebration. They had learned the importance of brotherhood that day.

Max and Fluffy

It was Max's birthday. He was really excited to meet all his friends and open the gifts they had brought him. At supper time, Max's mom called all the children inside as it was time for the cake cutting ceremony. Everyone sang the happy birthday song and wished Max.

After everyone had left, Max rushed to the living room to open his presents. However, he could not find any present from his mom. He asked his mother politely if she had forgotten to get a birthday present. She replied "No I haven't". Then she took Max outside and gave him his gift. It was an adorable puppy.

Max hugged his parents in delight. He couldn't believe that his wish had come true. He had always wanted a puppy and now finally he was finally getting one. Max decided that he would call his new friend 'Fluffy'. Soon the two struck up a great friendship. Max loved his new pet. They would play together all day.

Max would ride his new red bicycle everyday and chase after Fluffy. The two were best pals. Max thanked his parents for the gift and learned how to value pets and care for them.

The Magic Wand

Once upon a time in a far away land lived a little boy Bruno. He was a happy go lucky boy who lived with his grandfather Master Cane. Bruno was a big believer in magic and fairytales. He had learned all about them from his grandfather who was a famous magician at that time.

One day all of a sudden Master Cane fell very ill. Upon hearing this, Bruno rushed back to the house to check on his grandfather, but he was nowhere to be found. Bruno was very scared when all of a sudden he heard a voice. He turned around to see a frog who told him that he was his grandfather. Bruno could not believe it but then the frog told him of the magic spell.

Master Cane had been turned into a frog after drinking the forbidden water and now Bruno must turn him back. Bruno quickly followed the instructions and opened the book of magic spells. He grabbed the magic wand and cast the spell to turn his grandfather back. It worked instantly and Bruno was delighted. He hugged Master Cane in excitement and vowed to never leave him alone again.

Timmy's Trip to the Store

Timmy was a curious boy. He always wanted to know how things worked and he loved helping his parents around the house. Surely, Timmy needed to get to the bottom of this. "Where does the food come from?" Timmy asked his mother, "from the grocery store Timmy", answered his mother.

The next morning when Timmy woke up he realized that his mother was getting ready to go to 'the grocery store'. He jumped into the car as his mom gave Timmy a smile and asked "ready to go?" Timmy was more than ready to finally see the store.

Timmy couldn't contain his excitement and ran up to the big red sign, pulled open the door and walked in with his mother. They seemed to have gotten everything on the list and were making their way to the cashier, where this cheerful, young lady stood behind the counter and greeted them as they came close to the counter. Timmy noticed that each item was being marked, and then the lady at the counter gave Timmy's mom the bill, she paid and they were on their way. Now every time that Timmy's mom goes to the grocery store, Timmy is sure to tag along.

The Piggybank Story

Peter was a young boy that had everything. Some even considered him as a spoiled brat! Why? Because every time Peter was unable to buy a toy that he just saw, or buy a new game, he would throw a temper tantrum. The next day, Peter and his mom got ready to go shopping. When they went to the mall, Peter saw another toy that he liked and begged his mom to buy it for him. "No!" replied his mother, "you already have enough toys, if you want something, help around the house and we will start giving you an allowance and you can save up to buy what you want".

After failing to convince his mother to buy him the toy they were heading back to the car. It was at that moment Peter noticed a little boy with a brightly colored pink piggybank. Peter out of curiosity went up to the boy and asked "why are you standing out here with this piggy?"

The boy smiled at Peter and said, "I'm trying to collect money so that I can save up and take it home with me and give it to my father so that he can buy food for us to eat." From that day Peter started saving. He found two piggybanks around the house and began putting money into it. After a week, when Peter and his mom went out again he grabbed the first piggybank and took it with him and to his surprise he found the same little boy standing there in the cold. Peter went running up to him and handed the piggybank and said "this is for you" and walked away.

The Princess Who Hated Bath Time!

Once upon a time, there was a beautiful princess who lived in the Kingdom of Happyville, her name was Arianna. She was the most beautiful girl in the entire kingdom. Everyone loved her because she was always happy, always had a smile on her face and she loved everyone around her. However, the Princess had a bad habit, she didn't like having a bath, even though the queen would give her one every night before going to bed.

One night the princess grew irritable about the idea of having a bath that night. So, she decided that she wasn't going to have a bath. When time came for her to have a bath she told the queen "No! I don't want to have a bath", this went on for hours, till the queen got tired and sent the princess to her room.

The princess was happy; she had avoided taking a bath that night. This shenanigan went on for a couple of days. One day the princess went to meet the people of her kingdom, but nobody came close to her or hugged her because little did the princess know, she smelled bad. The princess ran back to her castle crying and told the queen what happened and the queen said "That's the reason I tell you to have a bath every night." The princess that night went and had a bath, and found that people played, laughed and hugged her. From that day Arianna always took a bath before going to bed.

The Chicken and the 4 Ducklings

Mama duck had four baby ducklings. They lived by the river along with the rest of their family. One day, during a thunderous storm the baby ducklings got separated from mama duck. Mama duck searched and searched but the baby ducklings were nowhere to be found. The baby ducklings were scared but they stayed together and waited for morning to come.

In the morning, the 4 baby ducklings looked for their mother but couldn't find her. However, soon they saw a hen with her 3 baby chicks and started following them. The ducklings were hungry and tired after running around all day. The ducklings then saw the nest of the hen and after the hen left for work they joined the chicks and shared the meal.

The ducklings told their tale to the baby chicks who agreed to help them. As the hen returned she was shocked to see the ducklings but the baby chicks told her that they were lost. The hen promised to help them and started searching for their mother. After a while the ducklings eventually found mama duck. She hugged them in joy and happiness. Mama duck thanked the hen for help before returning home.

Luke the Hungry Fox

It was a beautiful summer's day as Marty the lion and Henry the bear went out for a picnic. They packed all their favorite food. Marty the lion brought chicken, bagels and pastries while Henry the bear plucked some berries, apples and bananas. They packed their picnic basket and set off on their way.

Along the way the saw Luke the hungry Fox. Everyone in the jungle knew that Luke was always hungry and ate everyone else's food. Marty quickly hid the food, but it was too late as Luke had already seen it. Soon Henry and Marty reached the mountain by the river where they planned to have their meal. After a while, Marty felt thirsty and left to get some water. Before leaving, he told Henry to look after the food. But Henry was so busy climbing a tree that he didn't listen. Luke the fox had followed them and was hiding in the bushes. As soon as he saw that both Marty and Henry were busy he quickly stole the food. Luke enjoyed a tasty treat that day and by the time Marty and Henry returned all the food was gone. They both learned a lesson to never leave their food unattended again.

Sarah and Richard go to the Farm

Summer Vacations had finally arrived and Mr. and Mrs. Johnson were ready for the farm trip with their two children. Sarah and Richard were really excited that their parents were taking them to Uncle Joe's farm for the first time. They could hardly wait to see all the animals at the farm.

Finally after a long journey the Johnson's arrived at the farm. Uncle Joe greeted them warmly and showed them to their rooms. It was already night time and the farm tour would have to wait till morning. In the morning, Sarah and Richard woke up and ran outside ready for a fun day ahead. Uncle Joe started the tour by making some fresh breakfast. Then they went to have a look at the animals.

There were cows, hens, pigs, dogs, ducks and horses. Sarah and Richard fed the animals and petted them. Uncle Joe also had a big surprise for the kids. He took them along for a horse ride. Sarah and Richard loved every moment of their trip. In the evening they had a barbeque dinner before saying goodbye to Uncle Joe. Sarah and Richard thanked mom and dad for a fantastic trip.

Millie the Fox comes to Town

Tom the fox was a taxi driver and an adventurer. When he heard the news of his fun loving Cousin Millie's arrival he was delighted. He had been waiting for her to come to town for days. Finally, the day had arrived so Tom quickly got dressed and got in his trusty old cab, ready to pick her up and show her around town.

Tom happily drove to the airport in his black and yellow cab. After waiting for a while he finally saw Millie, she was dressed in a red outfit. She waved at him as Tom put her things in the trunk of the car.

Then Tom took her on a journey of fun and adventure. They went out for lunch in the afternoon, and then they went shopping and later in the evening they went to the park. After a long day, Tom and Millie returned home. Tom's mom and dad met Millie and gave her their best wishes before she returned. At night, Tom went back to the airport to drop Millie off. Millie thanked Tom for a wonderful day of fun as she waved goodbye.

Arthur the Brave

Once upon a time in a land far away lived a young sailor by the name of Arthur. He was known for his bravery and people used to call him "Arthur the Brave". One day the King called the people of the kingdom and asked for their help. He offered 500 gold coins to anyone who would bring back his ship that had been captured by red Indians. Upon hearing this Arthur stepped forward and accepted the challenge.

The King informed him of the dangers that he would face, but Arthur was not afraid. He promised the king that he would bring back the ship and the people who had been captured. The king made him commander of the team and gave him 100 men for the task.

Arthur came up with a clever plan to deceive the red Indians. He planned to send a few unarmed men at first to draw out the enemies and then the rest would attack from the sides of the island. The plan worked perfectly as Arthur and his men were victorious. They took back the ship and returned to the kingdom. Upon his return, the King showered him with praise and gave him the gold he was promised. Arthur proved that if you are brave anything is possible.

The Greedy Sailor

Alex was the most cunning sailor in the village. One fine day Alex hatched a plan to fool the villagers and steal all their money so that he could buy a new ship. He knew that the villagers were short of food so he asked them to give him money to buy food for them. Although Alex was not a trustworthy person, the villagers knew he was the only hope for them.

After taking the money, Alex set sail and travelled across the sea. Eventually he reached another island and then instead of returning back with food he used the money to buy a new ship for himself. Alex had broken the trust of the people.

Years later Alex returned to the same village with his fleet of ships which he had bought with the stolen money. He was now a successful trader but the villagers had not forgiven him and they hoped for his downfall. As he was leaving the village his ships got caught in a storm and were destroyed. He lost all his valuables and was poor again. We can learn from his experience that if you do wrong with others you will get punished for it sooner or later.

Roger's Dream

Roger was big baseball fan. He had always enjoyed playing the game with his dad at home, so when the trials for the school team were announced he was super excited. Roger's dad, Mr. Karl, had always encouraged him to play baseball. He knew his son was an excellent player. But Roger himself wasn't too sure about his skills and wasn't sure why he was overlooked for the team the year before.

But this year he was ready after having practiced hard on the pitch with his dad. Finally, the day of the trials came and Roger was feeling a bit nervous. He was afraid that he would fail again but Roger's dad told him that if he believed in himself he would play well and get selected. At last it was Roger's turn to face the pitcher so he readied himself as he walked onto the field. Feeling confident after his father's encouragement, Roger stepped up confidently as the pitcher threw the ball. He smashed it for a home run. It was an incredible moment for Roger who had finally lived his dream. The coach instantly selected him for the team. Roger proved that if you believe in yourself, anything is possible.

The Evil Pirate

Once upon a time there lived an evil pirate. He was conqueror of the seven seas and ruler of the land. One day an informer told the captain pirate that there was gold on a new found island. Upon hearing this captain pirate's eyes lit up, he had all the gold in the land but he wanted more.

Finally the captain pirate set sail ready to find some more gold. After reaching the island he sent all his men in different directions to search for the gold. But the gold was nowhere to be found. When he returned back to the shore all the ships had left. The Captain pirate was angry and could not believe he had been deceived by his own people. He was left alone on the island.

The Evil pirate had always mistreated his people and used them for his own advantage. Eventually, the people grew frustrated and overthrew him so that they could live in peace. The evil pirate's greed and vengeful attitude towards others had cost him. We can learn from the pirate's mistakes and make sure that we never take advantage of others.

The Light House

Rachel had always dreamed of visiting the light house but she didn't know that her first visit would be so adventurous. It was a beautiful sunny day as Aunt Molly prepared lunch for the family. Rachel was visiting her aunt for the weekend. After lunch Uncle Peter suggested that they visit the nearby museum. Everyone agreed and they were on their way. However, midway through the journey they realized that they had forgotten to bring the camera.

Since the house was only a short distance away Rachel agreed to walk back and get it. However, as she got near the house she could see smoke, she started running and as she reached the doorstep she saw that the house was on fire.

Rachel knew that there was no time to waste so she rushed to the shore and took the boat to the light house. After reaching the light house she ran upstairs and rang the alarm bell. She then used the lights to alert the authorities. Soon the message reached across and the fire brigade came over to put out the fire. Uncle Peter and Aunt Molly thanked Rachel for saving their house. Rachel proved that all you need is courage to help others.

Little Jack's Big Adventure

Little Jack was a sailor just like his father Mr. Arnold. He had spent most of his life sailing across the seas. Little Jack's best friend Ken was also part of the ship crew. Both friends were great explorers and would often find hidden treasures. One day they came across a rare gemstone. They found it on a treasure hunt on the forbidden island.

Since no one was allowed to visit the forbidden island, Jack knew that he couldn't tell his father about his discovery so he decided to keep it a secret. The gem was worth a lot of money and Jack knew that he couldn't hide it for long. Ken encouraged him to tell the truth as it would be best for everyone. Finally one day Ken decided that he would tell his father so he approached him in his cabin and explained the entire story.

Ken's father was very disappointed. He scolded both the boys for hiding the secret. But later Mr. Arnold realized that the boys had told him the truth and punishing them would be wrong. So he decided to let them keep the gem. This shows that if you speak the truth you will be rewarded.

The Flooded Castle

King Jeremy woke up to bad news in the morning. His informant told him that his castle had been flooded overnight and they were trapped inside. They couldn't get out because the water would drown them. King Jeremy was left helpless so he gathered his people and asked them for advice. A wise old man suggested that they must send out ravens with messages to the other castles and ask for their help. After pondering for a while, the King agreed.

The ravens returned and the messages were good. The other kingdoms had agreed to help King Jeremy. After a few days a few hundred men arrived outside the castle they analyzed the situation but couldn't find a solution and so they returned. The King in a desperate attempt to save his people offered a reward of 500 gold coins to anyone who would save the castle. The very next day a magician showed up and accepted the king's challenge. He instantly cast a magic spell to turn back the flood and save the people. The water was all gone, but before the king could thank the magician, he had disappeared.

Santa's Gift

Christmas was just around the corner and Louis was really excited. He couldn't wait to meet all his cousins. Louis had also made a special wish for Christmas, he wrote to Santa asking for a "Cho-Cho train". His parents were taking him to grandma's house this Christmas to celebrate.

Louis could hardly wait for morning to come. He slept at night thinking about his present and in the morning to his delight his wish had come true. Grandma woke him up and took him downstairs to open the presents. Louis ran but before he could open his present his mom asked him to sit down for breakfast. After breakfast it was finally time to open the gift. Louis took the red wrapping paper off the box and opened it. It was a "Cho-Cho train" just like he had wanted. Louis was very happy that his wish had come true. He hugged his mom and dad before he started playing with his toy. The train was amazing as it had lots of sounds and was remote controlled as well. Later Louis found a note in the box from Santa. It was a thank you note saying "Thanks for writing to me I hope you liked the present."

The Boat Race

It was again time for the annual boat race at Haleyville School. Liz and Maggie were best friends who had been competing in the race for years but had never won. However, this year they had special motivation as the reward for the winners was a hot air balloon ride. It was something that they had always dreamed about. At last it was time for the race.

With victory on their minds they set off and took an early lead in the first leg of the race. As they progressed further down the river their speed slowed down as they struggled to handle the difficult course. Soon they were behind and their arch rivals the champion team of Jamie and Elle had taken the lead. Going into the last stage of the race, Liz and Maggie did not lose their determination and they eventually pulled through moving ahead of Jamie and Elle just before the finish line. They had won the race. It was a magical moment as the two best friends celebrated. They were then given their prize; a ride on the hot air balloon which they thoroughly enjoyed. This just goes to show that if you are motivated no task is impossible.

Max the Smart Cat

Max was a furry cat that drank milk and ate cookies. Clark and his pet cat Max were best friends. Max was a very smart cat, he even helped Clark with his homework. Clark was lazy and did not like studying so he asked Max to do his homework for him. But one day mom found out and she scolded Clark but he did not listen.

But soon enough Clark would learn his lesson. It was time for the school exam and this time Max couldn't help him. Clark was on his own, but since he had not studied he failed the exam. Mom was not happy and she asked Max the cat for help. Max agreed to help mom. He told Clark that he would not do his homework anymore but instead he would teach him to do it himself. Clark had learned his lesson and accepted Max's help. Together they studied and learned. Now Clark was ready to take the exam again, he went back to school and this time passed. Mom was delighted with the result and she thanked Max. We learned from this story that we must never rely on others for our own work. We should do it ourselves.

The Runaway Cookie

Farmer Jones was in the market one day when he met a trader. The trader offered him a jar of magical cookies. The trader told him that if he put the cookies under his pillow he would never feel hungry again. But he also warned him that he must never eat the cookie or else he would be in trouble. After thinking for a while, farmer Jones finally bought the cookie jar from the trader and returned home.

He told his wife about the magical cookies but she did not believe him. So at lunch they ate all the cookies except one. At night farmer Jones put the one cookie that was left under his pillow and the next day he wasn't hungry.

Days went by and he wouldn't feel hungry. But one day a villager got to know about his secret. He told the rest of the people as well and then they planned to steal the cookie from farmer Jones. Later that evening the villagers entered the farmer's house while he was out in the fields. As soon as they found the cookie they wanted to eat it but the cookie started running away and was soon out of sight.

Jane the Elephant Doctor

Little Jane loved animals and she cared for them a lot. One day while she was out in the jungle with her friends she spotted an injured elephant. She quickly rushed over to help it. The poor elephant was badly hurt and was crying. Jane looked at him and saw that its trunk was damaged. She asked the elephant to lie down so that she could treat him.

Jane quickly rushed back to the camp where her friends were. She told them about the elephant and its injury. They agreed to help her and all of them went along with her back to where the elephant was. Jane had brought along her medical kit which she would need to fix the elephant's injury. Jane then quickly took out a bandage and wrapped it around the elephant's tusk. Her friends then fed the elephant and after that it stopped crying. The elephant was now happy that Jane had fixed its injury. He thanked Jane and her friends for their help before giving them a ride back to their camp. Jane waved goodbye to the elephant and this completed another day in the jungle for Jane and her friends.

Donald's Farm

Donald was a hard working farmer. He had a beautiful farm with lots of animals. One day while returning from the grocery store he saw a man enter his farmhouse. Donald quickly rushed to check what was going on. Upon inspection, Donald found out that his beloved chickens had been stolen. He couldn't believe his eyes. He asked the neighbors if they had seen his chickens but no one had a clue.

Donald was very sad at losing the chickens, but then his friend Louis came up with an idea to get the chickens back and catch the thief. He suggested that they catch the thief by tricking him. So the next day Donald and Louis cleverly hid themselves behind the bushes and waited for the thief to strike so they could catch him. It was afternoon time and finally a man in a black coat appeared. He was heading for the ducks this time but before he could make his move Donald and Louis caught him. They called the police who took away the thief. Donald and Louis had done it, they got the chickens back. Donald was really happy and thanked Louis for his help.

Jenny Gets Lost in the Forest

Jenny was out with her friends in the jungle, doing some exploring when she heard a loud roar. Jenny's friends Sarah and Mike started running, they asked Jenny to follow them but she was too tired and couldn't keep up with them. Soon she was lost. Jenny was scared because she did not know the way back home and her friends had already left her.

But Jenny was a brave girl. She decided that she would not cry and would look for a way home. It was almost night time when Jenny heard some animal sounds. She moved closer to the noise and found out that there were some sheep that were eating grass. She went towards them and looked at them. The sheep stared at her for a while but looking at her innocence they decided to help her. She told them that she had gotten lost in the forest and did not know how to get back. Since it was night time the sheep told her that they should search in the morning for her friends.

Ryan's Day at the Beach

Ryan the explorer was an adventurous kid. He was very outgoing and fun loving. So when Uncle Tony called him up to spend a day at his beach house he couldn't resist. It was summer time and Ryan was looking forward to a good vacation. Ryan packed his things and waited for his uncle to pick him up. Uncle Tony finally arrived in his shiny new car and picked him up. Ryan had also brought along Spike, his pet dog.

Along the way Uncle Tony told Ryan that he had a surprise for him as well. Ryan was super excited and couldn't wait to see what Uncle Tony had planned for him. After reaching the beach house, Ryan took Spike for a walk outside. The weather was beautiful and it was a perfect summer's day. After returning from the walk Ryan asked Uncle Tony what the surprise was. Uncle Tony then told him that he was taking him for his first ever fishing trip. Ryan was delighted. He had been waiting for this moment for a long time. The two of them returned at night after the trip. Ryan had caught his first fish. He thanked Uncle Tony for the wonderful experience before returning home.

Skittles the Cat Takes a Bath

Skittles was a dirty cat. He didn't like taking baths and would always smell bad. Other cats did not like to sit with him but Skittles didn't care. However, one day everything changed for Skittles the cat. He was lying around when his cousin told him that mama cat was coming to visit him. Skittles was very scared of mama cat. He knew that mama cat would not be happy to see him dirty.

Skittles decided to fool mama cat by spraying himself with perfume, but still the smell wouldn't go away. He even bought new clothes but still Skittles was very dirty. Finally it was the day of mama cat's arrival so Skittles decided to hide and told his cousin Suzie to tell mama cat that he was not around. But Suzie was tired of Skittles being dirty all the time so she decided to tell mama cat about Skittles. Mama cat was not happy with Skittles and asked him to take a bath right away. Skittles quickly jumped in the bathtub and cleaned himself. After a while, he came out looking all refreshed. He was a clean cat now, mama was happy. Skittles promised to take a bath everyday from then on.

Steve's New Neighbor

Steve and Michelle were best friends. They were also neighbors since childhood. Both friends would play together all day long. But one day a new girl Maria moved into the neighborhood. She was very friendly and caring. Steve quickly became friends with her while Michelle was away on vacation with her family. A couple of months later Michelle returned and instantly went to Steve's house to meet him but he wasn't there. She was surprised so she asked Steve's mother Mrs. Johnson where he was. She told him that he had gone out to play with Maria the new neighbor.

The next day Michelle met Steve but he wouldn't talk to her. Instead he went over to Maria's house. Michelle could not believe that his best friend had changed in such a short time. The two stopped talking, but then one day Steve was riding his bike when he fell off and got injured. Michelle rushed to save him and took him to the doctor. Later Steve thanked Michelle for her help and apologized. The two agreed to be friends again. Since then, Maria, Michelle and Steve became best friends and played together every day.

Tubby the Racing Hamster

Tubby the hamster and his friends were watching TV one day when the mailman arrived and told them that there was a car race coming up next weekend. Tubby was a big fan of car racing although he had never won a race, but after hearing about the prize he couldn't resist. The winner was going to get a free trip to wonderland. It was Tubby's favorite place in the whole world.

Tubby prepared for the race with the help of his buddy Robbie. They both started by looking for a car for the race. After a while Tubby came across a beautiful red car. It was very expensive, but Tubby knew that he had to win the race and he needed a fast car to do so. After buying the car, Robbie ad Tubby returned home. They waited for the weekend to arrive and then finally it was time for the race. Tubby was determined to win, he started his shiny red car and went ahead full speed. He jumped barriers along the way as he finally reached the finish line. Tubby had beaten the rest and clinched victory. He was going to wonderland to fulfill his dream.

Mickey the Lucky Farmer

Mickey was a farmer. He lived in the town of Clarksville along with his brother Timmy. Both brothers were hard working but they were also very poor. One day a thunderous storm destroyed their farm. The two brothers had nothing left and they were very sad. However, the very next day Mickey met a trader in the market who offered him special magical beans. The trader claimed that the beans would fix his farm instantly.

Although Mickey did not trust the trader, he knew that it was the only choice. He returned home having bought the beans. Mickey then told his brother about the incident but Timmy was not happy because Mickey had spent all their remaining money on the beans and now they had nothing left. Mickey decided that he would still give it a try. He planted the beans in the ground at night and the next morning their glorious farm had returned. It was even better than before, Mickey and Timmy were delighted. They could now finally earn some money. The brothers decided that they would help the needy and poor with the money they had earned and live happily together.

Jessica's Visit to Grandma's House

Little Jessica was planning to visit her grandma for the weekend. She lived far away in a forest by the lake. Jessica had always wondered why her grandma lived so far away, she was eager to find out. Mom packed Jessica's clothes for the trip and wished her good luck on the journey as she left home. Jessica left in the morning and took the train towards the village. After reaching the village she began her walk towards the forest where grandma lived.

Jessica was amazed by the beauty of the forest. The birds were singing and the sun was shining bright. Soon she reached grandma's house. She greeted Jessica warmly and invited her inside. It was Jessica's first trip to grandma's house and she was really excited. Grandma then made her lunch and told her about how she decided to live in the forest. Jessica then went out and explored the wonderful forest. She made friends with some animals before returning inside at night. Grandma then made dinner for her after which she went to sleep. The next day Jessica returned home and told her mother of her wonderful adventure. She wrote to grandma and thanked her for a delightful weekend.

Captain Cook's Last Adventure

Captain Cook was a great sailor, he was known across the seven seas for his bravery and courage. One day he met a wise old man who told him about an island far away. The old man told him that the island was full of treasure and valuables. Captain Cook had gotten very old by now but he was ready for one last adventure. So he set sail with his crew to search for the lost island.

However, after days of searching he still couldn't find the island so he returned home disappointed. But then a magician told him that the island could only be seen at night. Captain Cook trusted the magician and once again set sail with his men. He waited for night to come and then all of a sudden in the distance he could see the lost island. Captain Cook eventually arrived at the island and it was full of gold as he had been promised. The captain was delighted, he asked his crew to gather all the gold. Soon they were on their way back home with all the gold. Captain Cook finally decided to retire after his last adventure.

Little Johnny's Night with the Spider

Little Johnny was always attracted to spiders. Every morning he would go out into the garden to search for little ants that he would pick up and keep in a matchbox. Little Johnny liked to drop the tiny ants in the web and watch as the spider quickly darted out from the corner to meet her feast.

One day, Johnny was caught by his mother. "What a terrible thing to do!" She exclaimed. "You are a bad little boy" she scolded as they walked up the stairs to the bedroom. "You have been a bad little boy today" she said as she shut the bedroom door behind her.

"What a terrible state the poor ants must be in," he thought as he dosed off to sleep. That night he woke up to a strange sound coming from somewhere in his bedroom. It was dark and Johnny could not see properly as he got up and looked around curiously. As soon as he turned around, he felt something leap on his back. "What was that," Little Johnny shrieked as he darted across the room dropping his torch on his way towards the door, but to his surprise the door would not budge. It was locked from the outside.

"Let me out," he shouted as he could hear the footsteps of the spider move towards him. The creepy footsteps grew closer when all at once, he heard a voice……….. "Rise and shine," He opened his eyes and to his delight it was mom, come in to wake little Johnny up for school. Thank goodness, it was only a dream, he thought to himself.

The Boy Who Thought He Could Fly

Adrian was a very popular boy at school. His friends had a lot of fun with him because he was very outgoing. One day Adrian decided that he would do something that would amaze everyone at school. He wanted to impress all the boys and girls so that he would become more popular. So he came up with a plan to deceive everyone. He decided to dress up as a superhero and trick everyone.

The next day Adrian showed up at school wearing his glimmering new costume. Everyone was surprised to see him. They asked him to prove that he had super powers. Adrian knew that he didn't have any powers, but still he told them that he could fly.

Now it was time to prove it. So Adrian got up on the roof and jumped without thinking twice. He thought he could fly but he couldn't. Adrian fell to the ground and injured himself badly. He was immediately taken to the hospital for treatment. Adrian was laughed at by the entire school who thought he was really foolish to attempt something like this. This shows that you shouldn't try to trick anyone because it will only do you harm.

Sarah Gets a New Cat

Sarah was roaming around the neighborhood one day when she suddenly heard noises of screaming from the back alley. She quickly ran towards the sound thinking that someone was in trouble and needed help. As she reached the alley she saw a beautiful little cat lying on the ground. It was hurt really badly and needed medical help. Sarah rushed back home to get her medical kit then she came back over to fix the cat.

The cat had fallen badly and hurt its back. Sarah took her back home and nursed the cat back to health. They both became great friends, and Sarah decided to keep her. Sarah named her Lilly and from that day on they played together every day. Sarah told her mother that she had decided to keep the cat as a pet. Sarah's mother was proud of her for performing such a good deed. Sarah had always wanted a pet cat and now she was finally getting one that loved her. Sarah and Lilly continued their friendship and lived happily ever after. This shows us that if you perform good deeds you will always get something good in return.

The Rat Pirates

Kyle the rat and Marty the rat were both pirates. They had one thing in common, they both loved cheese. One day an old mouse told the pirates that there was plenty of cheese on a far away island. Upon hearing this, both the pirates Kyle and Marty readied their troops and set sail in hunt for the cheese. Midway through the journey the two faced off against each other.

Both wanted the cheese for themselves. After reaching the island they started fighting and eventually a battle started between the two groups. Marty's pirates took the right side of the island while Kyle and his shipmates went to the left side. The cheese was lying at the top of a mountain and there was only one pirate who could have it. After fighting for days, both Kyle and Marty called a truce, they decided that there was no point in fighting. Instead they could share the cheese. So all the rats climbed up on to the mountain and saw that there was so much cheese that it could last a lifetime. The fighting was only a waste of time. Both Marty and Kyle decided to become friends and share everything from then on

The Great Escape

Cesar the conqueror and his troops set sail in search of a new land where they could settle. A priest had told Cesar about a beautiful tropical island located towards the north side. However, Cesar feared that the island would already be occupied and they would not be welcomed by the settlers. Soon Cesar's fears turned out to be true. As Cesar's ship reached the island they were instantly attacked by local villagers.

Cesar and his men were outnumbered by the villagers who took over the ship and captured them. They were then taken on the island as prisoners. The local villagers asked them why they had come. Cesar told them that they just needed a place to live as their old island had been flooded. But the villagers were not convinced, they thought that Cesar had come to attack them and take over the island. Despite Cesar's best efforts to bring peace, the villagers would not let them leave. Then Cesar decided to come up with a plan. He started a fire that distracted all the local villagers and in the meantime Cesar and his men escaped. They showed bravery to take back their ship and return to the sea.

The Hungry Elephants

Ross the elephant was very friendly and good natured. He always helped others in their time of need. One day Ross was very hungry so he came back home to eat but mama elephant told him that they had run out of food. The entire elephant family had nothing to eat and nowhere to go. Ross was shocked to hear this so he decided to ask a friend for help. Ross went over to Paul the monkey's house who told him that there was plenty of food across the river.

Ross then came back home and told the family about the news. Papa elephant agreed to travel in search of food. They all left together in the morning and walked towards the river. Ross' baby brother Albert was really tired but they knew that they had to continue so they did. Days had gone by since they started their journey but eventually they reached their destination and found the food. The entire elephant family was delighted, they ate hungrily and filled their tummies with food. Ross the elephant was happy and he had learned that sharing is caring. If you help others they will help you in return.

Baby Tiger Goes to Town

Baby tiger was growing up fast and mama tiger knew that he was ready for his first trip to the town. So on a Sunday afternoon mama tiger decided to take baby tiger for a trip to explore the town. As they left home, baby tiger began to wonder what the town would be like. He soon saw bright lights and tall buildings as they went about. Mama tiger promised him that it would be a wonderful experience and that they would have a lot of fun.

First, mama tiger took baby tiger to the circus then they had lunch at a restaurant. Baby tiger loved the sushi and the ice cream. Then in the evening mama tiger took him skating. Baby tiger had lots of fun over there as well. At the end of the day mama tiger and baby tiger went over to meet some friends. They stayed there for a while and had dinner before finally returning home. Baby tiger loved his first day in the town. He thanked mama tiger who promised him that they would return again soon for another trip.

Tommy the Lazy Cat

Tommy the cat loved sleeping. He lived alone in the big city and spent his days eating and relaxing. One day he got a call from his grandpa who told him that he was coming over to visit him for a week. Tommy was very surprised as he wasn't expecting any guests. Tommy's house was a big mess and he knew that it needed cleaning or else he would be scolded by his grandpa.

As Tommy did not know how to clean up himself he asked a friend for help. Martha the neighborhood cat came over to help him. She suggested that they buy some new stuff as most of the furniture was in bad shape. So the next day Tommy and Martha went to the market and bought what was needed. They came back to see that grandpa had already arrived and he wasn't pleased to see the house. He got mad at Tommy and told him to clean it up right away. Tommy began working and by bedtime the place was fixed. Then Tommy had dinner with grandpa who told him the importance of staying clean and not creating a mess in the house. Tommy had learned his lesson and promised to keep his house clean always.

Tony the Cat goes to the Doctor

Tony the cat hated doctors! He was afraid of needles and would always find excuses to avoid visits to the doctor. But one day he fell very ill and his mother asked him to get ready to go to the doctor but he refused. He was very scared and hid in the closet so that he wouldn't have to go.

Tony's mom and dad were worried, they searched everywhere but couldn't find him anywhere. Eventually Tony's friend Peter found him and convinced him that he must see a doctor.

Tony's mom and dad then drove him to the doctor's clinic. Soon they reached the clinic and took a seat outside waiting for the doctor's call. Tony was still very nervous but he was very sick and couldn't fight it any longer. Finally it was Tony's turn, he went inside and the doctor greeted him warmly. He told Tony that there was nothing to worry about. The doctor started the checkup and diagnosed the problem. He gave Tony some medicine and told him that he would be alright in a few days time. Tony was relieved, he was back to full health and up to his usual mischievousness in two days time and his fear of doctors was gone!

The Town Sale

It was again time for the annual town sale but Andy the mouse was not ready. He had not planned anything for the big day of the year. Suzie was very worried because only two days were left for the festival. She called Lizzie the fox for help and she immediately arrived with her cousin Paul. The two were known as big problem solvers and would always find a way out of troublesome situations.

This situation was a big problem but Lizzie quickly came up with a plan. She got everyone together and told them what they had to do. Andy the mouse would go to everyone's house in town and collect the stuff they wanted to sell. While Suzie would manage the decorations, Lizzie and Paul would pack the stuff and take it to the yard. Despite being short of time they eventually managed to pull it all together and prepare the yard for the town sale. The next morning people from all across town rushed in to buy stuff. By evening they had managed to sell everything thus concluding a successful town sale. Lizzie, Andy, Suzie and Paul celebrated their team success with a wonderful dinner party which was much appreciated by the people of the town.

The Art Competition

Sally was a very lively girl. She loved two things the most, the first was playing with her cat Skittles and the second was drawing. Sally had always been fond of art and when she heard about an art competition at school she couldn't resist taking part. Sally told her mother about the competition and she was also very excited. She encouraged Sally to practice every day so that she would be ready in time for the contest.

Sally really wanted to win the competition and she began practicing from the very next day. She drew plants, animals and buildings and showed it to her art teacher at school. The art teacher was really impressed with her work and wished her good luck for the contest. Finally the day of the competition had arrived and Sally was ready. The contest had attracted a huge crowd and Sally began feeling the pressure, but she knew that if she concentrated on her own work she would win. After an hour the contest was finally over and it was time for the results. Sally had her eyes closed as the judge announced her name. She was delighted. Sally won first place in the competition and thanked her teacher for believing in her.

Ben and Leslie's Treasure Hunt

Little Ben and Leslie were ready for their weekend beach trip with their mom and dad. They quickly got dressed and sat in the car, ready for a fun day ahead. Dad drove the family to the beach, it was a beautiful day and the sun was shining bright. Leslie and Ben ran out of the car to explore the beach as mom and dad took out the stuff from the car and set it up.

Soon it was lunch time and mom called Leslie and Ben to eat. After lunch mom and dad took a nap while Leslie and Ben went about exploring the beach. Soon they came across a cave, Ben couldn't resist going inside while Leslie followed him. Then they came across an old box. It looked like a treasure chest. Leslie got her flashlight and opened it. Both Ben and Leslie were shocked to see that the box was full of gold and jewels. They had actually found treasure. Ben rushed back to tell mom and dad but they didn't believe it. But when they saw the treasure they too were amazed. Mom and dad then told the police of their find who then let them keep the treasure.

Skippy the Dog goes on a Train

Skippy was the most popular dog in town. He knew how to have fun and that is why everyone liked him so much. One day the people of the town asked Skippy for help. The town party was coming up and they were short of food so they needed someone to go and get food from the neighboring town. Skippy was always up for a challenge and he agreed to go.

One thing that Skippy didn't know was that he would have to travel by train. He had never been on a train and he was really scared. He thought about giving up but his cousin Marty convinced him that he would have a lot of fun. So after a while Skippy packed his things and was ready for his first train trip. He went to the train station and eagerly waited for the train. Eventually the train arrived and the adventurous Skippy jumped on. He was very excited, and after a day's journey he returned with the food. The people of the town were delighted to see him. Skippy had a great time on the journey. He thanked the town's people for choosing him as this was the most fun he ever had.

Toby's Halloween Party

Toby loved candy and Halloween was his favorite holiday. This year he was really looking forward to Halloween as his uncle Jimmy was coming over for the holidays. Toby was busy decorating his house for the big day when he heard his neighbors call him. Toby rushed over to see what the matter was. Mr. Johnson told him that they needed someone to decorate their house as they were going away and would return on Halloween.

After thinking for a while Toby agreed to help his neighbors. However, Toby knew that he wouldn't be able to collect candy with his friends if he decorated Mr. Johnson's house. So the very next day Toby started with the decorations while his friends went out to collect candy. Finally by night Toby was done decorating the house. It looked beautiful. The Johnson's returned and were delighted with the decorations. They appreciated Toby's work and as a reward gave him a huge bag full of candy. Toby thanked Mr. Johnson before returning home. He then told his friends about his day and they were really happy for him. Toby had managed to get more candy than all of his friends. This goes to show that if you help others you will be rewarded.

Edward the Boy Wonder

Edward was an orphan that was part of the crew of Captain Cook's ship. Edward was very adventurous and brave, but people did not take him seriously since he was orphan. But Edward was not disheartened, he believed in himself and knew that someday he would prove himself to the world.

One day Captain Cook and his crew were out in the ocean when they encountered a pirate ship who wanted to fight them. Captain Cook tried to avoid the battle since he only had a few men.

Soon, a battle started and although Captain Cook defeated the pirates he had lost most of his crew and almost all of the food on board! The Ship was also in very bad shape. The Captain knew that they needed to find land fast or else they would be doomed. The Captain ordered Edward to start the search. Edward climbed to the top of the ship and spotted an island nearby. He then steered the ship towards the island. The Captain and his crew were safe. Edward looked after his shipmates and helped them recover. Captain Cook was so impressed by Edward that he decided to reward him with gold coins and named him the "Boy Wonder".

The New Teacher

It was another regular day at Parkville elementary school when Principal Higgins came in and announced that Mrs. Cruise was leaving the school and the third graders were going to get a new teacher. The students were not at all pleased because they loved Mrs. Cruise and didn't want her to go. However Principal Higgins told them that there was nothing he could do and that they should welcome their new teacher warmly. The students sat in the classroom as they waited for the new teacher to arrive.

Jimmy, the class monitor, wondered what the new teacher would be like while his classmates also started discussing the same topic. Soon they heard a knock at the door as the new teacher entered. She said hello to the class as the students gazed upon her. She introduced herself as Mrs. Michael. Then she gave a brief introduction about herself and then asked the students about their past experiences. The students were already beginning to like her. She was so relaxed and calm which made the students very comfortable. By the end of the day Mrs. Michael had won over the hearts of all the students. They adored her and accepted her as their new class teacher.

Tiny the Hungry Dinosaur

Tiny was a very small dinosaur but he ate a lot. One day in the jungle a fire broke out and all the food was burnt. There was nothing left to eat and Tiny was very hungry but he did not know what to do. Tiny's mother told him that he must search for food since everyone else was also very hungry. The next day Tiny the dinosaur left home early to look for food but even after a long search he couldn't find anything. So he returned home unhappy.

But then Tiny's friend Louis the lizard told him that he knew where the food was and that Tiny should follow him. The two of them then set on their way to find the food and after a while they eventually came across a mountain that was full of food. Tiny climbed to the top and called out the rest of his family. They all rushed towards the food and ate hungrily. Everyone was satisfied and thanked Tiny for his help in finding the food. Tiny had become a hero for everyone and they loved him for being the food finder.

Marshall and Jessica's Fishing Trip

Marshall and Jessica were really looking forward to their summer vacations as dad had promised to take them on a fishing trip. At last the day had arrived, both Marshall and Jessica were really looking forward to a great day of fun and adventure. Dad packed up the equipment and was ready to go. Marshall and Jessica got in the car as mom waved them goodbye. Soon they arrived at the lake where they would be fishing.

Dad told them that they should be careful. He gave them life jackets and instructed them to stay safe in the water. Dad then got out his trusty old boat and cleaned it up before they hit the water. Eventually they all got in the boat as dad paddled away. Finally they found a spot where they would stay and start fishing. Dad took out his fishing pole and after a while caught a fish. Marshall and Jessica were really happy that they had caught a fish. Dad then told them about his past fishing experiences and how he learned to fish. In the evening the family returned home to surprise mom who then cooked the fish and they ate happily.

The Pet Shop

Aunt Martha was a pet lover. She had two cats, two parrots and three horses. One day the town's council announced the opening of a new pet shop. Upon hearing this, Aunt Martha got really excited as she was looking for gifts to give to her nephews. She visited the pet shop the very next day. It was very crowded and Aunt Martha couldn't find what she was looking for. After leaving the new shop disappointed, she went to the market and that is where she discovered a small animal shelter.

Aunt Martha was amazed to see the adorable little animals. She knew that these animals needed to be rescued so she decided to get two for her nephews. She got a cute little piglet and a small kitten. She returned home with the two new pets she had got. The next day her nephews Joe and Mike were coming over so she decided to surprise them by presenting the pets as gifts. Joe and Mike loved their aunt's gifts and thanked her for such wonderful presents. Aunt Marta had managed to save these wonderful animals and given them a new home.

Rover the Rescuer

Robbie and his dog Rover were best friends. They played together all day long and had lots of fun. One day Robbie decided that they should go together to the jungle to explore. Robbie asked his mom if he could go, but she warned him that it was too dangerous and told him that he shouldn't go. But Robbie was up to mischievousness and the next morning when mom was out grocery shopping he sneaked out to go to the jungle along with Rover.

Robbie ran as he approached the jungle and without thinking twice he rushed forward. Rover was left behind and soon Robbie was lost. He fell over a ridge and injured himself. Robbie was lost in the big jungle and he did not know what to do. He called Rover for help and after a while Rover eventually found him. Rover then helped Robbie get up and the two of them returned home as night fell. Mom was really worried and she was happy to know that Robbie was fine. Robbie then told mom how Rover had saved him. Mom was very pleased with Rover and gave him a treat as a reward.

The Skating Championship

Drake was the town's skating champion and had been for quite some time. He had never lost a skating contest and was considered as the best skater in town. Drake however was a very naughty boy. He did not respect his elders and would often get into trouble. The annual skating championship was only a week away and Drake was feeling very confident, he didn't even practice thinking that he would be easily able to beat everyone. However, this overconfidence would cost him later.

Another boy in town, Mike, was also preparing for the big skating competition. He knew that he had very little chance of winning but he did not give up and practiced hard day and night. Finally the day of the skating contest was here and everyone was ready. Drake went up first and did very well. It seemed that he would win again until finally it was Mike's turn. He was determined to do well and win the championship. Mike earned a thunderous applause from the crowd as they were amazed by his performance. Then the results were announced and Mike had won the championship. Drake's overconfidence and arrogance cost him the championship.

Jack meets Uncle Simon

Little Jack had always heard stories about his great Uncle Simon, so when the opportunity to meet him came up he knew that he couldn't resist. Uncle Simon was a great explorer and was known all over the world for his bravery and courage. He was visiting town for the weekend and Jack would finally get a chance to see him in person. Jack was super excited and decided to dress the way his uncle dressed. Finally the day had come to meet Uncle Simon.

Mom drove Jack to the harbor where Uncle Simon was waiting for him in the ship's cabin. Uncle Simon warmly greeted Jack and offered him lunch. After lunch Uncle Simon took Jack on a tour of his prestigious ship. Jack was amazed, he couldn't believe that he was actually on Uncle Simon's ship. Uncle Simon then told Jack about his numerous adventures. Jack was very impressed with the stories he was told. Finally it was night time and Uncle Simon had to leave for his next adventure. Jack wished him good luck as he waved bye to his uncle. Jack returned home and told mom about his wonderful experience. It was a great day for Jack that he remembered forever.

The Big Storm

Another weekend was coming to an end and it was time to go back home. Dad thanked Aunt Kate for the excellent meal. Mom and dad sat in the car with Pete and Lilly to go back home. It seemed just like any other journey but then all of a sudden lightning struck and the weather began to change. Rain was showering down and it became difficult for dad to drive any further. So they stopped at a nearby gas station. Pete suggested that they should take shelter.

Mom and Dad agreed and they started looking for a place to take shelter and then they came across an old house near the river. They went inside and were greeted by a noble family who allowed them to stay till the storm would pass. The storm was very powerful and it caused havoc all night long, so the next morning the family hit the road again after the storm had passed. Dad quickly drove home and finally they were all safe. Mom and Dad appreciated Pete's clever thinking which had gotten them out of trouble.

The Lost Soccer Ball

Lucy and Dwayne were playing soccer like they did every Saturday when all of a sudden they lost their soccer ball. Lucy had kicked it really far and they couldn't find it. But after a while Paul the dog spotted the ball at the top of a tree. But the tree was very high and neither Lucy nor Dwayne could climb it. They wondered what to do but couldn't come up with a solution. But then Mr. Anderson their neighbor suggested that they should use a ladder.

Dwayne then quickly went inside and got the ladder but it was too heavy so he asked Lucy to give him a hand. Finally they managed to get the ladder outside. Lucy then set it up and Dwayne started climbing. It took Dwayne a while to reach the top since the tree was very high but he finally managed to retrieve the ball and then carefully climbed back down. Lucy and Dwayne then put the ladder back in the storehouse and carried on playing. They thanked their neighbor Mr. Anderson for his help. The two of them had learned a valuable lesson that day about teamwork.

The School Beach Trip

Tony and Toby were really excited with the school beach trip just days away. They had all sorts of plans in mind. Finally Principal Elliot announced the schedule for the trip and asked the students to come prepared on the weekend. Tony and Toby told their parents' about the trip who approved of it instantly. On Friday Tony and Toby packed their things as the school bus picked them up. Soon they were at the beach. The weather was amazing. The sun was shining bright and the wind was blowing.

All the students ran towards the beach and started playing. Tony and Toby were ready for a day full of fun and adventure. They started by building a wonderful sand castle and playing hide and seek. In the afternoon they had lunch and then continued with the day's activities. Soon it was evening and it was time to go back. The students wanted to stay but they knew that it was getting late. So everyone boarded the bus and left for home. Tony and Toby got back after an exciting day, they had a lot of fun and they shared their adventure with their parents who were happy for them.

The Town's New Road

Felix the fixer was called by the town's council one evening. They told him that the town's road needed to be reconstructed since it had gotten old and was no longer fit for use. Felix agreed to fix the road but warned that it would take some time. The council agreed to his demands. Felix and his team soon began working. Felix first inspected the damage to the road and found out that it needed a lot of work. So he got his team ready for the big task ahead.

Felix assigned everyone different tasks and told them how to go about their job. Soon a plan was in place and the work began. After days of hard work the road was finally fixed. All the people of the town were really excited to see the new road. They wanted to drive on it to see how it was. Felix then declared the road open and soon cars were driving on it. The people of the town were really happy because the road was of excellent quality. They thanked Felix and his team for their brilliant work.

The Noble Merchant

The village of Duckworth was a very peaceful place to live. The people of the village were very hard working and almost all of them were farmers. One day a vicious flood destroyed the entire farmland and all the crops were gone. The farmers had no food to eat or sell and they were in a lot of trouble. But then one day a noble merchant came to the village. He was very ill and needed help. The farmers took him in and nursed him back to health.

After the merchant had recovered he asked the farmers if there was some way he could repay them for helping him in his time of need. The farmers then told him about the flood and the damage it had caused. The noble merchant agreed to help them. He told the villagers that he was a very successful trader and belonged to a wealthy family. The merchant gave the villagers money in return for their help so that they could rebuild the farmland and once again live on their own. The villagers were delighted. They thanked the noble merchant for his help and told him that he was always welcome back again to the village.

Ralph's Winter Vacation

Ralph loved the winter season. It was one season of the year that he looked forward to the most. This year he was again going to visit his Aunt Mary on his winter holidays. Ralph was super excited because he knew he would have a lot of fun. On the weekend mom drove Ralph to Aunt Mary's house where he met his cousins Phil and Jerry. The three of them were best buddies and would do all sorts of activities together.

This year they had planned to go ice skating for the first time and Ralph was really looking forward to it. But first they needed to buy the skateboard and safety equipment. So Aunt Mary drove the three boys to the local sports shop where they bought the equipment and then returned home. In the afternoon Aunt Mary made lunch and all of them ate hungrily before getting ready to go ice skating. Finally it was time to go outside and have some fun. Ralph and his buddies had a great time all afternoon. They made a snowman and played in the snow all day long. Ralph returned home at night and thanked Aunt Mary for a wonderful winter vacation.

The Mayor Comes to Town

Mayor Lucas' return to town was only days away and Mrs. Smith was very worried. He had gone on a business trip to another village and left her in charge. The town had become a mess nothing was in order as Mrs. Smith was busy taking care of her nephews. She just couldn't find the time to do the duty that was assigned to her. But now she knew that some action needed to be taken or else the mayor would not be pleased.

Mrs. Smith instantly called a meeting the next day at the town's council office and asked the council members to help her clean up the town. Soon a plan was in place to clean the dirty town and fix the roads. Mrs. Smith worked all day and eventually she managed to pull it off. The town looked amazing. Everything had been fixed in a short time. The next day Mayor Lucas finally returned. He was delighted to see that the town had been maintained so well even in his absence. He thanked Mrs. Smith for the wonderful job she had done and even offered her a reward for her hard work.

Kevin's First Baseball Game

Kevin's grandpa was a great baseball player of his time. He always told Kevin stories of his playing days and how he had become a star. This got Kevin really excited and he became a fan of the game. His favorite team was the "Mudville Warriors", a local team for whom his grandpa had also played. One day grandpa told Kevin that he had been invited to a Mudville game as a special guest and he was taking Kevin along with him to watch the game.

This got Kevin really excited because he had always wanted to watch a game. So the very next day Kevin got dressed all ready to go to the game. Grandpa told him that they needed to make it there early so that they would get the best seats in the house. Grandpa drove the car and eventually they reached the stadium. Kevin was amazed to see the huge stadium and the large number of fans there. At last the game began and it was a real nail bitter but in the end "Mudville" succeeded. Kevin was really happy he had just experienced his first baseball game. He thanked grandpa for taking him along for a wonderful trip.

Travis the Fool

Travis was a very foolish person. He was a very selfish animal catcher. One day he set about catching some monkeys in the jungle. He wanted to trap the monkeys by tricking them. But that day he was the one who would end up being fooled. Travis started off by making a plan to trap the monkeys. He thought that he could trick the monkeys by putting out some bait and when they would come to get it he would trap them. However the monkeys were a lot cleverer than Travis.

As Travis entered the jungle, he set up some traps and left banana as bait. He then waited in his car for the monkeys to come out but they didn't. Travis thought that there was something wrong with the traps so he went back in to the jungle to look at them. But then the monkeys attacked. They pushed Travis and he tripped falling into his own trap. Mud was all over his face as the monkeys laughed at him. The monkeys then quickly grabbed the bananas and escaped. Travis had been fooled by the monkeys. He returned home and promised to never do such a thing again.

The Lost Puppies

Antonio had three cute little puppies, Bruno, Tina and Scruffy. He loved all of them and would play with them all day long. One day Antonio forgot to lock the house while leaving with his family and on his return the puppies were gone. Antonio was really worried, he searched everywhere but the puppies were nowhere to be found. Antonio asked his dad to help him. Dad called the police and told them about the situation. The police chief agreed to help and immediately sent out his team to search for the puppies.

Antonio worried about the safety of his beloved puppies. He asked his friend Sarah for help who agreed and at night the two of them went out to look for the puppies. After a while they heard a noise from the nearby park. Antonio rushed over and called out for his puppies. He had finally found them. They were playing in the park. Antonio grabbed all three of them and took them back home instantly. He told mom and dad about the search mission and they too were happy that the puppies were back. Antonio promised that he would not repeat such a mistake again and would always be careful.

The Old Scientist

Once upon a time, an old scientist had a little pet dog, named Ponzo. One day the scientist left his room, leaving his pet dog asleep in front of the fire place.

For over twenty years, the old scientist had been hard at work, studying the most difficult problems you could imagine and on the table lay the sheets of paper in which he had written down all that he had found out during that time.

When his master, the scientist, was gone, little Ponzo got up and looked all around. His master was nowhere to be seen so he jumped on the table and overturned a lighted candle. At once, all the papers caught fire and were soon reduced to ash.

Just then the old scientist opened the door of the room. He saw that all his hard work had been destroyed by the fire, and there stood little Ponzo, happily wagging his little tail from side to side.

Almost any other person in a fit of rage might have, or would have gotten very angry at the poor puppy. But the old Scientist had a kind heart and patted his pet dog gently on the head, although his heart was filled with sadness and grief.

The Good Cobbler

Benjamin was a cobbler, and was never rich. Though he never had enough money to live happily, he longed to own a wagonette of his own. A wagonette is a horse-drawn vehicle for two people and to be able to buy one Benjamin saved up every penny he could which he then kept in a wooden box under his bed.

He had saved a $100 when one day a friend and humble neighbor, who was a poor man, came to his house and told him in tears that he did not have any bread to give his children, all their furniture had been taken away and they had no place to go.

Benjamin had a good heart and at once stood up and went towards his wooden box.

"How much do you need," he asked his friend.

"A hundred dollars," the friend replied.

"There you are, now go and get some food to eat and pay to get your furniture back," said Benjamin as he emptied all his savings into the man's hands. The next day another friend came over and asked him, "What will you do now about the carriage you wanted to buy, Benjamin?"

"My friend," replied Benjamin with a soft voice, "I shall continue to go on foot, as it is much less important for me to have a carriage than for my friend to have food."

The Shadow at the Edge of the Garden

It was in the happy month of December when Ben, his friends Paul and Sean and his brother Ralph used to sit every night after dinner and talk about the lovely things they were expecting as presents from their parents and relatives. On 19ᵗʰ Dec, they had just finished putting up some of the decorations and it was rather late, about 11 p.m. It was one of those exciting and cold nights and they sat curled around the fireplace where they were sipping their tea, when all of a sudden Ben's brother, Ralph, shouted and said there was a ghost in the house.

"LOOK BOYS!" said Ralph pointing at the figure in a distance. They all looked and did see something that was dark, walking across the wall. After hearing all the noise they made, their father came out and asked them what was wrong. Just as they were pointing out to him towards the wall where they had seen the shadow, he said "Yes, I can see something going to and fro near the wall. Come on boys let us go and see."

Ben, Ralph, Sean and Paul were too scared to follow their father to the wall. However, when their father got near, he turned around and shouted to the boys that were standing at a distance. "You silly boys", He said, "come here and see the ghost you saw." It was a stray cat that had scared the boys. As the cat was walking by, its shadow was cast on the wall which looked as if it was a ghost. After that day, the boys learned that they should never jump to conclusions.

Lee the Famous Fisherman

Lee was an expert fisherman. He was known in the village for his fishing skills. However Lee was getting old and was about to retire. The people of the village requested him to train someone before he retires so that his skills would not be lost. Lee agreed to the villagers request and set about picking his successor. The very next day Lee met a young boy named Chen who was very enthusiastic about fishing. Lee was very impressed with his attitude.

Lee told the villagers that he had selected his successor and would train him. Chen was really excited about being given the opportunity. He thanked Lee for choosing him. However Lee warned him that the training would be very tough and he better be prepared. Chen was not deterred by the challenge, and was excited about learning from the best. Lee first told him how to spot a fish and the bait that he used. The first stage was all about observing but then later Chen himself had a go. At first he struggled but with time he got better and was ready. Lee announced his retirement and encouraged Chen to carry on and continue serving the village.

The Great Horseman

Diego was one of the finest racers of his time. He had won many horse races and was considered the best in the land. But one day a man came over to Diego's village and challenged him to the legendary "Pony Express Race". The race would take place in the deserts of Africa across the rocky terrain. It was considered as one of the toughest races of all time. Diego had never competed in it, but he was not one who would back down from a challenge.

Diego accepted and began preparing for the race. Diego's horse Hidalgo was the fastest horse in the land but he had never run a desert race. Diego was worried that his horse wouldn't make it but his friends convinced him to participate. At last the day of the race had arrived and Diego was ready. Diego raced ahead of the rest at the start but then the heat began to affect his performance and he slowed down. But Diego was not one who would give up easily he charged ahead in the last leg of the race and moved ahead of his rivals to win. Diego became a legend that day because he won the "Pony Express Race"!

Robert and the Story of the Eggs

Robert was a happy go lucky rabbit. He hoped around all day eating his favorite carrots. Robert was also a great singer and would regularly perform at the local club. One day while returning from work, Robert found some eggs lying on his front porch. He did not know what to do with them so he asked his neighbors if they knew who they belonged to, but no one had an answer. Robert decided to keep the eggs with himself for the night.

The next day Robert left his home early with the eggs to search for the rightful owner. Down the road a hamster told him that the eggs belonged to Lucy the hen and she had been looking all over for them. Robert quickly rushed over to the hen's house but she wasn't home. Lucy had gone out to look for her eggs. Robert decided to leave the eggs in a basket with a note saying that he had found the eggs and was now returning them. Lucy the hen returned after a while and was delighted to see her eggs. She went over to Robert's house and thanked him for his help.

Daniel's Piano Lessons

Daniel was a very talented young boy. He loved music. He would listen to it in his spare time and often play the piano as well. Daniel's mom and dad were very proud of his talent and encouraged him to pursue music. Daniel's school music teacher told his parents that they must consider piano lessons for him as he was an excellent piano player. Daniel's mom and dad agreed and they immediately hired a piano teacher.

Daniel was a bit scared at first as he did not know what the piano teacher would be like. But when she arrived Daniel was very happy. The piano teacher was very charming and she loved kids. Daniel was learning quickly and improving his skills. He quickly became an accomplished piano player. The teacher encouraged him to participate in the upcoming school contest. Daniel did brilliantly in the talent show and won the prize for Best Performance! Everyone was impressed with Daniel's performance. Daniel returned home and thanked his teacher for believing in him. He had realized his potential and now wanted to be a musician. Mom and dad agreed to Daniel's request by letting him follow his dream.

Printed in the USA
CPSIA information can be obtained
at www.ICGtesting.com
LVHW081927230224
772668LV00006B/736